To: Na
From:
April 2018
Barb

Written by Joe Fitzpatrick Illustrated by Marco Furlotti

Designed by Flowerpot Press
in Franklin, TN.
www.FlowerpotPress.com
Designer: Stephanie Meyers
Editor: Katrine Crow
DJS-0912-0156
ISBN: 978-1-4867-0946-5
Made in China/Fabriqué en Chine

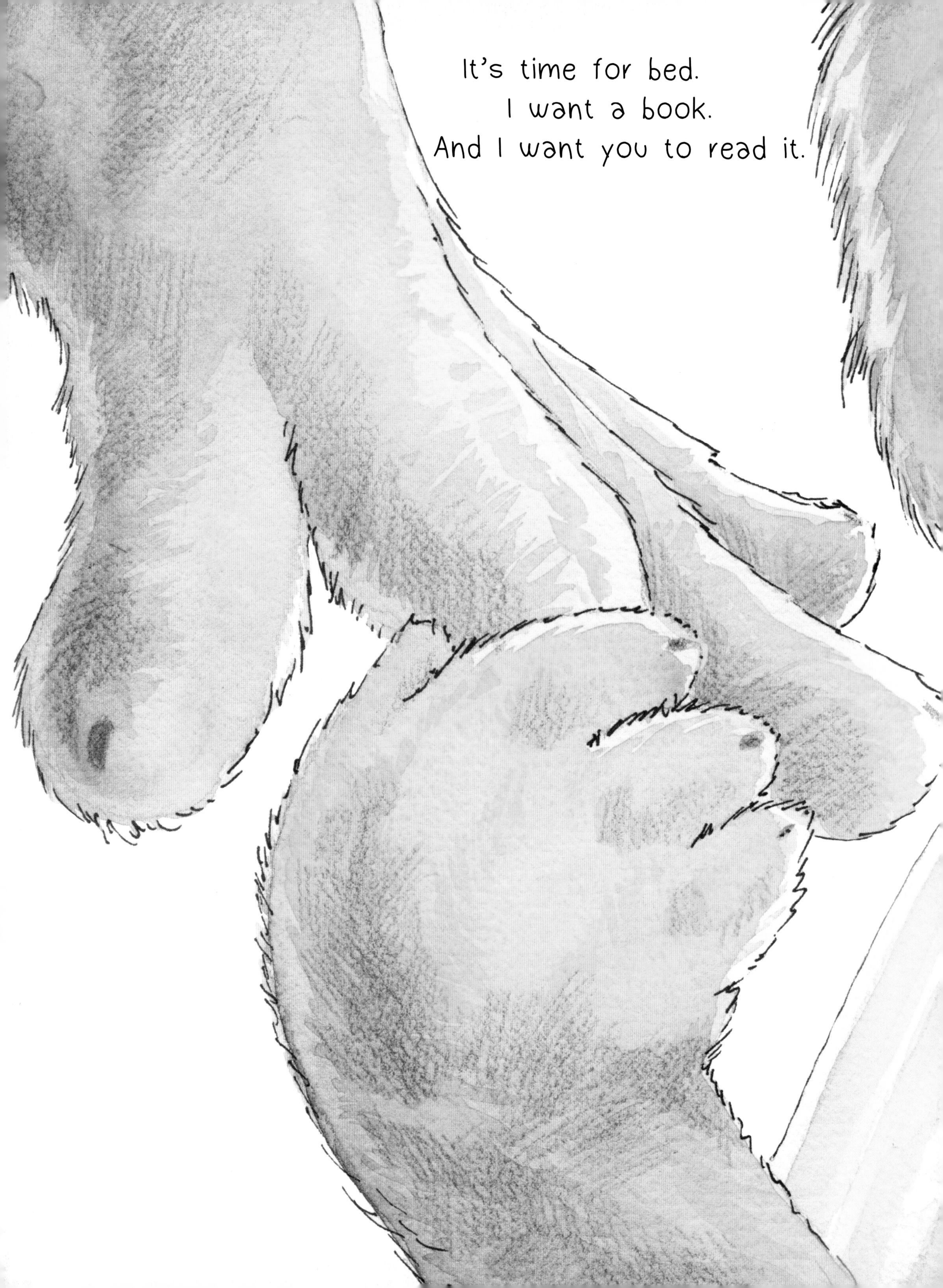
It's time for bed.
I want a book.
And I want you to read it.

But listen close to my advice,
you are gonna need it.

This book is not like other books
that we have read before.

It looks the same as normal books,
but it has one rule more...

Whisper when you read this book.
It's safer when you're quiet.

One time I read this book out loud
and that started a riot.

Whisper when you read this book.
If others want to hear...

have them cuddle in real close,
then whisper in their ear.

Whisper when you read this book.
It makes the book more fun.

It also means I listen close
until the book is done.

Whisper when you read this book.
I won't make a peep.

Don't worry if my eyes are closed.
I am not asleep.

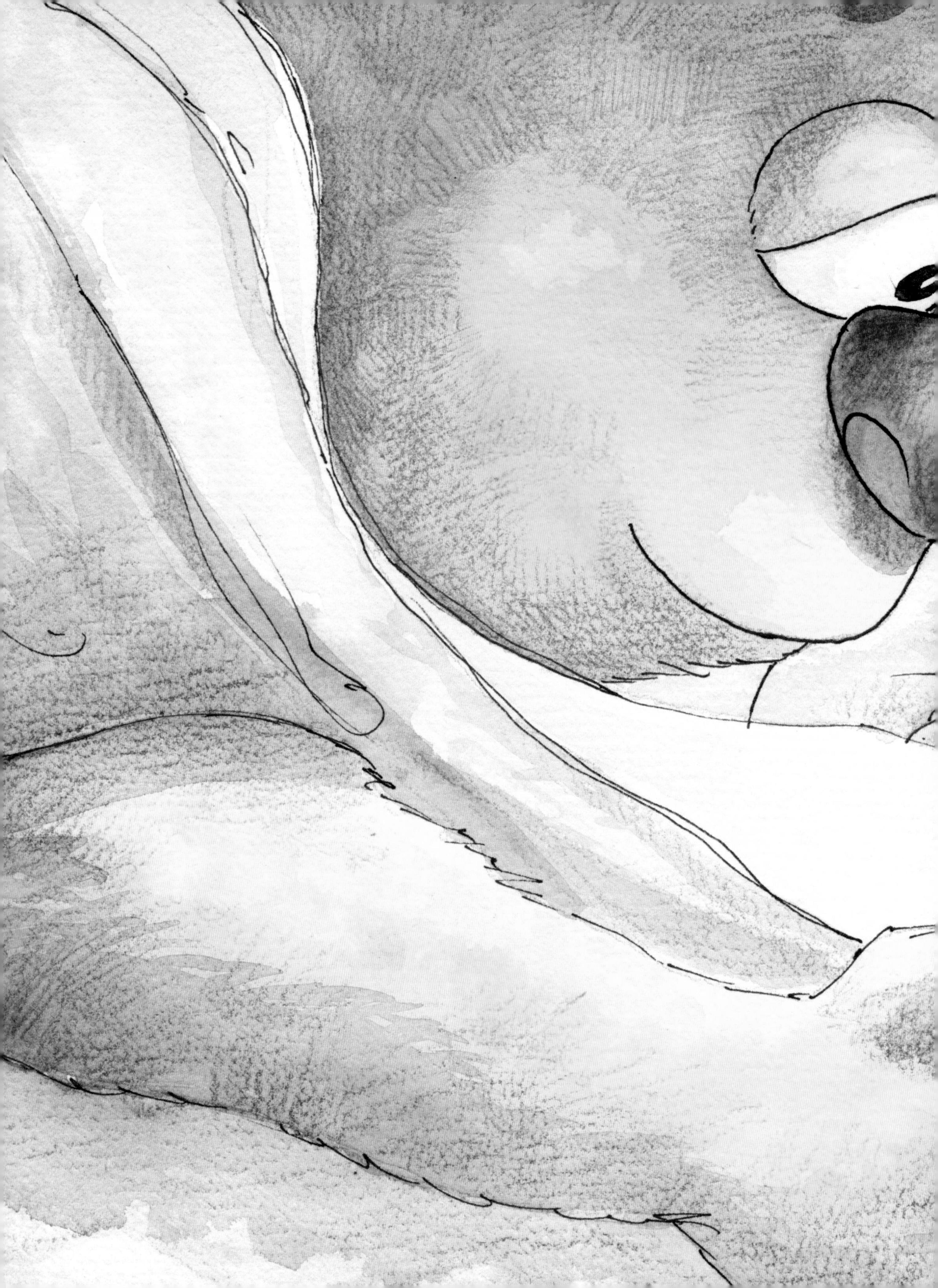

Whisper when you read this book.
Get in nice and tight.

And when you're done
say "I love you,"
then kiss my head good night.